Dedicated to Love

Published by The Art of Joy Publications
First Published 2016
Text © Stella Joy 2016
Illustrations © Tara Joy 2016

All Rights Reserved
No part of this book may be reproduced in any form by
photocopying or by any electrical
or mechanical means, including information storage and
retrieval systems, without permission in
writing from the copyright owner.

ISBN 978-0-9956110-0-9

For more information about ordering and other publications
Please contact: theartofjoypublications@gmail.com

A Traveller's Tale

by **Stella Joy**

with illustrations by **Tara Joy**

Come join Pam Pan on her journeys withher old friends the owls and the pussy cat
Please feel free to bring more life into the pages by colouring them in

Pam Pan – daughter of Peter the eternal youth- is one of life's travellers. Her journeys have been wide and diverse and full of turbulence and wonder. Through this little book she shares some of the insights that she gained along the way, in the hope that they can inspire us to hold to our dreams in those inevitable moments when we feel overwhelmed by the pressures of life.

traveller's tale

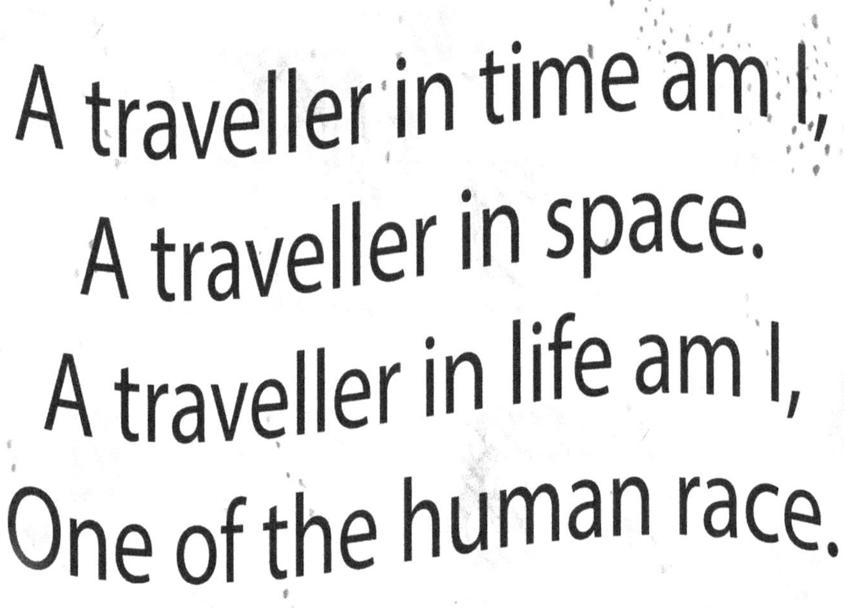

A traveller in time am I,
A traveller in space.
A traveller in life am I,
One of the human race.

HEART OF GOLD

Space and time I've travelled,
Whether still or moving fast.
In house, or truck, or tipi,
Life moves me on my path.

HEART OF GOLD

Through experiences it moves me,
Through choices made each day,
Experiencing Love in action,
Experiencing fear and pain.

LOVE
in action
FEAR

An angel and a demon,
They've spoken in my brain.
One spoke words of wisdom,
One spoke words of gain.

FLY WITH LOVE

One spoke of Liberation,
Of Love and Joy and Peace.
The other said "you're mad, a dreamer,
You should face reality!"

One said
"Reality's what you make it,
What you go for in your life.
You're alive now...
Yet for how long?
Live what you Love most.
What's the use of strife?"

The other said "No, follow me!
You're a loser if you try
To live the life of Love...
In poverty you'll die!".

"Nothing will happen to you...
You'll rue your life, you'll lose,
Regard my power! Don't think so much,
Accept ME!
Don't even choose!"

A traveller in time am I,
A traveller in space.
I knew I had the power to choose
Which way I turned to face.

HEART OF GOLD

To face my highest visions,
My deepest dreams within,
The Angel's face of beauty,
The child-like ways of seeing.

Or face the world of nightmare,
Reflected all around,
People's fears projected into
A world of sight and sound.

The Angel whispered *"Love is all"*
And you know…this is the Truth!
Follow your heart, it opens ways
To realise the dreams of youth.

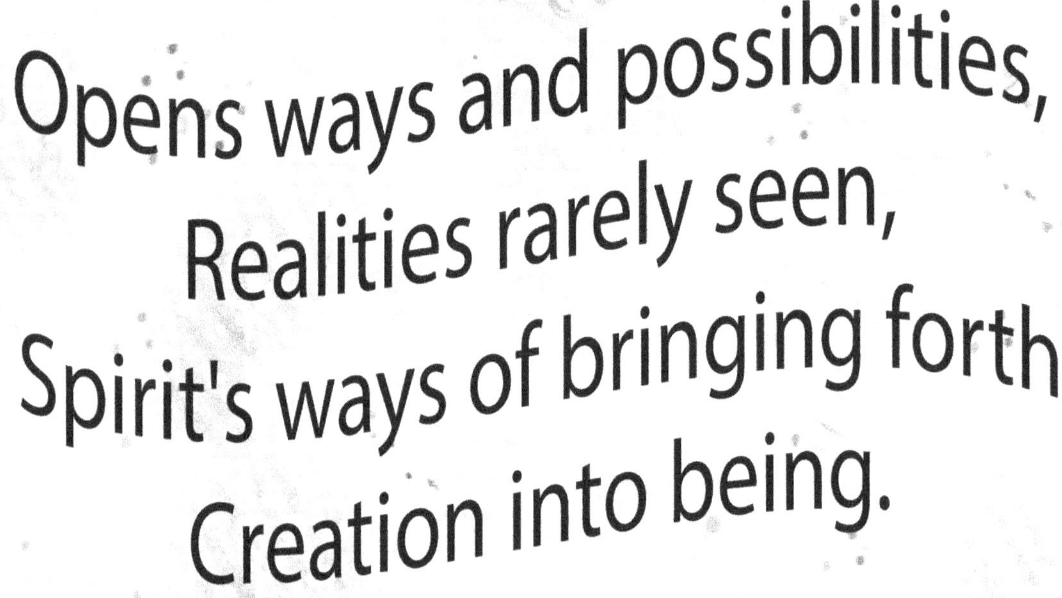

Opens ways and possibilities,
Realities rarely seen,
Spirit's ways of bringing forth
Creation into being.

I've heard the cacophony of demons,
I've heard the Angel's quiet voice within,
One shouted *"LIMITATION!"*
One whispered *"bright freedom"*.

So I've chosen the way of Love
And have much of Love in life,
For Love grows Love and more of Love
And moves us beyond strife.

The choice to Love brings freedom
As it opens up our eyes.
The path of Love is hard but true
And is not limited by lies.

So listen to your bright dreams,
They'll wash away your fears,
As you bring them into being,
As you live them through your years.

Travellers in time are we,
Travellers in space,
Travellers in life are we,
Some of the humans…

Some of the humans… Being.

HEART of GOLD

Thank you for your support!

All profits from the sale of this book go to
support the work of Active Remedy Ltd,
a non-profit UK based organisation focused
upon safeguarding the global water cycle through
promoting and aiding mountain ecosystem
restoration and conservation projects globally

www.activeremedy.org.

So listen to your bright dreams,
They'll wash away your fears,
As you bring them into being,
As you live them through your years.